LIBY
ROTHERHAM
S66 8LD

Musical Beds

For Marissa, Eva and Jonathan
but especially for Martin and parents everywhere
M.B.

For Maura, Linde and Hilke
M.P.

ROTHERHAM LIBRARY & INFORMATION SERVICES	
B48 1329735	
Askews	
YC	£4.99
	R00043645

POCKET
BOOKS

First published in Great Britain by Simon & Schuster UK Ltd in 2002
Africa House, 64–78 Kingsway, London WC2B 6AH

This edition first published in 2003 by Pocket Books, an imprint of Simon & Schuster UK
Originally published in the USA by Simon & Schuster Children's Publishing Division, New York in 2002

Copyright © 2002 by Viacom International Inc.
Text copyright © 2002 Mara Bergman
Illustrations copyright © 2002 by Marolein Pottie

All rights reserved

A CIP catalogue record for this book is
available from the British Library

ISBN 0-7434-6208-4

1 3 5 7 9 10 8 6 4 2

Printed in Singapore

Musical Beds

Written by Mara Bergman
Illustrated by Marjolein Pottie

POCKET
BOOKS
London • New York • Sydney

Josie could not sleep.

The moon was too bright.

The old tree shivered and shook in the light.

"Daddy!" she called. "Come here quick!

There's a witch in my room!"

Dad came upstairs.
"Don't worry," he said.
"It's only the apple tree
making shadows on the wall."

He pulled the curtains tight
and kissed Josie good night.
"Go to sleep now," Dad said.

But Josie could not sleep
so she slipped across the landing
to Mum and Dad's room.
The room was dark
and there were no scary shadows.

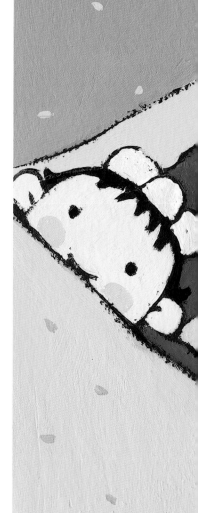

Josie slipped into the big bed
and crawled between the soft sheets.
Soon she was fast asleep.

Rosie could not sleep.
The room was too cool.
and something called

Whooo! Whooo! Whooo!

"Daddy!" she called. "Come here quick!
There's a ghost in my room!"

Dad came upstairs.
"Don't worry," he said.
"It's only the wind
whistling through the apple tree."

He shut the window tight
and kissed Rosie good night.
"Go to sleep now," Dad said.

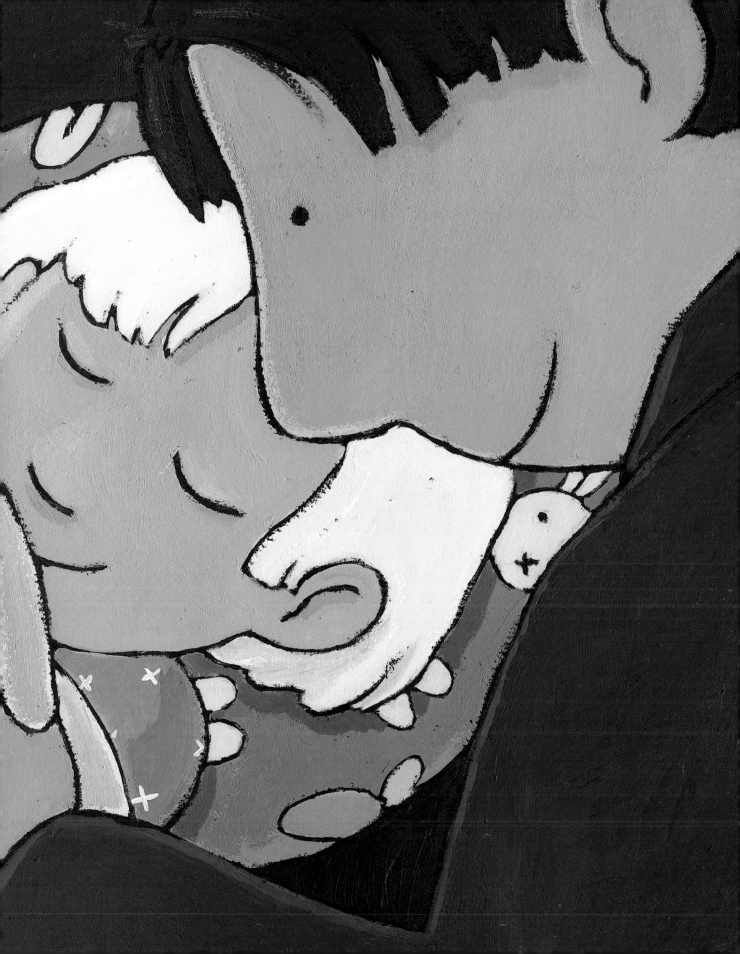

But Rosie could not sleep
so she slipped across the landing
to Mum and Dad's room.
The room was cosy
and there were no scary noises.

Rosie slipped into the big bed and
crawled between the warm sheets.
Soon she was fast asleep.

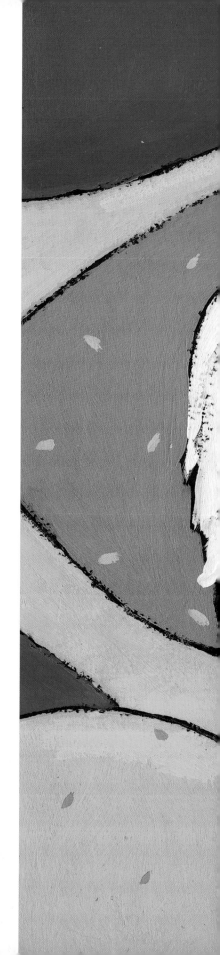

Little Rick could not sleep.
"I'm thirsty!" he called.

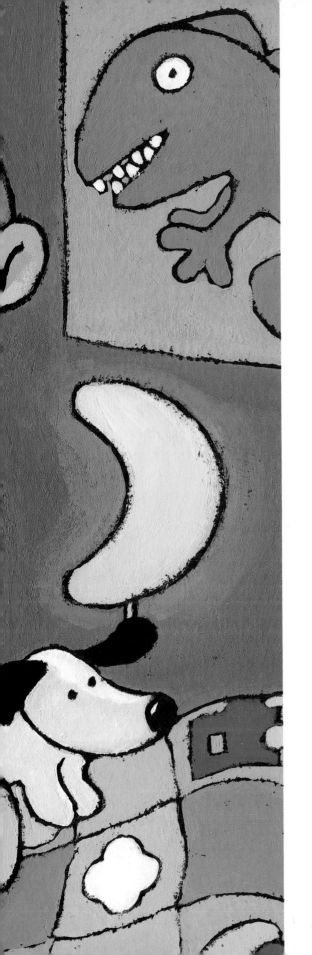

No one answered
and no one came
so he bounced

down the

stairs on

his bottom.

Dad gave little Rick a glass of water,
then carried him back to bed.

"Go to sleep now," Dad said.

It was Dad's turn to sleep.
There was no room in the big bed
so he went to Rosie's bed,
in the bottom bunk.
He was reading his book when . . .

Little Rick came in.
"Daddy, I can't sleep, I'm lonely!"
Little Rick climbed into bed next
to Dad . . .

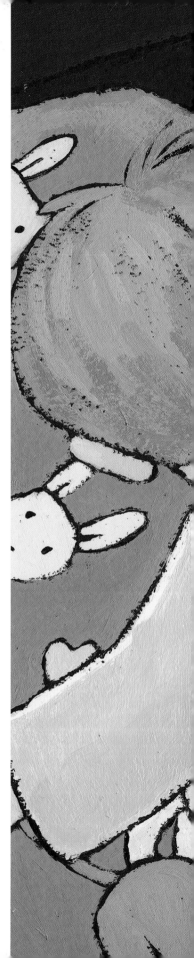

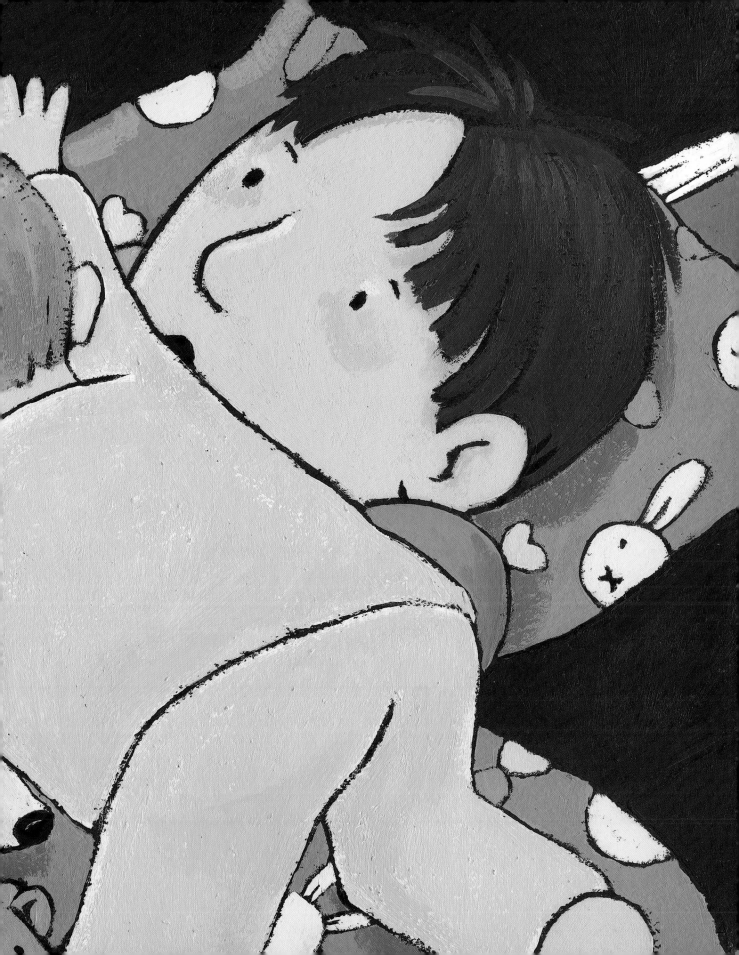

. . . and soon he was fast asleep.

But Dad could not sleep!
Little Rick kept kicking him
and pushing him.
Dad could not sleep
so he climbed to the top bunk.

But it was full of cuddlies and
books and pointy puzzle pieces
and besides . . .
Dad wanted to sleep in his own bed.

There was only one thing to do!

First he carried Little Rick
back to his own room.
He put Doggy and Monkey and Lion
all around him
so he wouldn't be lonely.
Little Rick slept, snug as a snail.

Then Dad carried Josie back to her bed.

There were no scary shadows and no witches.

Josie slept, cosy as a caterpillar.

Next, Dad carried Rosie back to her bed.

There were no scary noises and no ghosts.

Rosie slept, quiet as a carrot.

Then Dad read in
bed for a few minutes
before he, too, fell
fast asleep . . .
tired as a turnip.

When Mum came home
she gave everyone a
good night kiss.
First Josie, who was cosy
in the top bunk,
just where *she* belonged.

Then Rosie, who was quiet
in the bottom bunk,
just where *she* belonged.

Then Little Rick, snug
in his own room,
just where *he* belonged.

Then Mum got into her bed
next to Dad, feeling very pleased
that everyone would sleep,
comfy as kittens,
peaceful as pandas . . .

. . . at least until morning!